Little Bridge Farm

Dilly Saves the Day

Dilly the duckling is frightened of EVERYTHING! But life's not much fun when you can't join in your friends' games – will Dilly always be a scaredy-duck?

Look out for all the Little Bridge Farm books!

Little Bridge Farm

Dilly Saves the Day

PETER CLOVER

Illustrated by Angela Swan

SCHOLASTIC

First published in 2007 by Scholastic Children's Books
An imprint of Scholastic Ltd
Euston House, 24 Eversholt Street
London, NW1 1DB, UK
Registered office: Westfield Road, Southam, Warwickshire, CV47 0RA
SCHOLASTIC and associated logos are trademarks and/or registered
trademarks of Scholastic Inc.

10 digit ISBN 0 439 94465 1
13 digit ISBN 978 0439 94465 6

British Library Cataloguing-in-Publication Data
A CIP catalogue record for this book is available from the British Library

Printed in the UK by CPI Bookmarque, Croydon, CR0 4TD
Papers used by Scholastic Children's Books are made from wood grown in
sustainable forests.

5 7 9 10 8 6 4

www.scholastic.co.uk/zone

To Jan and Paul

Chapter One

It was raining heavily. Water gurgled down drainpipes and into water butts outside Big Red Barn. Inside, the barn was warm and cosy and bustling with noisy young animals.

Old Spotty cleared her throat.

"Today, I'm going to tell my story from inside the barn. It's too wet to sit beneath the Telling Tree." The sow raised her voice above the excited chatter. "Quieten down now, please," she oinked. "Small animals at the front, bigger animals at the back. Let all the little ones through!"

Dilly watched as Tiger the kitten wrestled with her brother for the last seat on the cat blanket. A stream of yellow chicks bustled over to a pile of hay and made themselves comfortable, peeping quietly. Smudge the Labrador puppy settled down at the front of the crowd.

"Is that everyone?" Old Spotty asked, impatiently. "Dilly! You can't see from back there. Move up, quickly. I'm about to begin my story."

Oscar the young pony moved aside to let Dilly waddle past.

"*Quack!* Excuse me, please. Can I squeeze through?" Dilly pushed her way to the front, trying not to feel too awkward as everyone watched her. She found a place to sit and shook out her wet feathers.

"Hey! Watch out, Dilly," squawked a gosling.

"Oops, sorry," said Dilly, lowering her head. She gave a final wriggle, waving the fluffy feathers in her tail. Part of Dilly's tail had been bitten off by a nasty fox when she was only a baby, and now

there was a bare patch.

"Harrummpphhh! Ooof!" Old Spotty clambered up on to the square bales of hay set up as a platform in front of her audience. She pulled her trotters beneath her belly, and settled down in a wobbly heap. Then she flapped her leathery ears and everyone fell silent.

Dilly held her breath, waiting to hear the story.

"The Willow Farm Feather Race," began Old Spotty, "takes place every year." Dilly knew all about the Feather Race between the ducks, the swans and the geese. And in two days, they were going to hold the race again. Her brother, Racer, was taking part this time.

Dilly could feel a question building up inside her. Normally, she would never dare interrupt Old Spotty. Dilly was far too shy to call out. But this time… If she didn't get her question out, she'd burst!

"Is the race as dangerous as everybody

says it is?" Dilly asked, thinking about her brother.

"Old Spotty doesn't like interruptions when she's about to tell a story," whispered Parsley, the tiny Jack Russell terrier.

"I know," Dilly quacked softly. Then she whispered quietly in Parsley's ear. "But my brother, Racer, is swimming this year. I want to know that he's going to be OK."

Old Spotty raised one white eyebrow and fixed Dilly with an icy stare.

"It's not as dangerous as all that. We wouldn't let youngsters race if it was. Now, if you've quite finished asking questions AND whispering among yourselves," grunted the pig. "I was about to tell you the story. You DO want to hear the story, don't you?"

"Oh yes! Yes! Yes!" exclaimed Parsley.

Old Spotty began again. "The Willow River Feather Race takes place every year, and the greatest race of all time was many, many years ago. That year, the contestants – Goldie the gosling, Silver the swan and Drake the duckling – had trained hard for the race for weeks. But the favourite to win that year was Silver the swan – she was by far the fastest cygnet on the river. There had been a lot of rain that week…"

Dilly listened hard. Dilly had never swum in the Feather Race herself, or ventured past White Stone Bridge – she was far too nervous. But she knew every centimetre of the course.

"The rain had made the river extra fast that year," said Old Spotty. "Rock Falls is the trickiest part of the race. And with all the extra water, it had become a raging torrent."

"Here comes the best bit," whispered Dilly to herself.

"The race was feather to feather all the way," said Old Spotty. "Drake Darefeather reached Rock Falls and swam the Gushing Gap to beat Silver the cygnet and Goldie the gosling by a beak's length! Drake the duckling won the race in style, claiming the trophy for the ducks."

"My granddad!" Dilly said. She looked over her shoulder at Drake, who stood at the back of the crowd. He gave Dilly a wink and she ruffled her feathers with delight. Dilly loved her granddad very much.

Dilly looked back at Old Spotty.

"And that was the last time that the ducks won the annual race. Every year since, the swans or the geese have taken the Golden Feather Trophy." Dilly could feel another question tickling her – just one last question that she had to ask.

"Who do you think will win this year?" Dilly called out, trying to make sure that her voice didn't tremble.

Old Spotty twirled her corkscrew tail. "This year," she announced, "all three swimmers look strong: Racer the duckling, Swift the cygnet and Glory the gosling. It could easily be anybody's race!"

The three contenders looked proud as they sat in the front row with their heads held high.

Dilly waved to Racer. The little black duckling winked at her.

Then Old Spotty called out, "Three cheers for the Willow River Feather Race."

All the animals cheered, from the little chicks in the front row to the giant shire horses at the back. The hens clucked, the dogs yapped, the kittens yowled and the piglets squealed.

"Hip, hip, hoorah! May the best bird win!"

Chapter Two

That evening, just before sunset, the rain finally stopped. "I think a practice run would be good," Old Spotty said to Racer, Swift and Glory. They waddled after Old Spotty out of the barn and towards Willow River. Dilly watched them leave. She didn't want to be left behind when there was a chance to watch Racer swim the river! She sneaked out of the Big Red Barn and followed the three birds.

"Where are you going?" called a voice. Dilly turned round. It was Socks the piglet. Behind him stood Monty the moorhen. They both looked keen to join in with Dilly's fun! She waved a wing towards them.

"Come on," she said. "I'm going to watch the practice run." Her friends ran to catch up with her and they followed Racer and the others towards the river.

"The race starts from here," said the old sow, "from White Stone Bridge, and ends, downriver, at the Old Tree Stump overlooking Rock Falls."

Dilly and her friends peered over the side of the bridge.

"All this rain has made the river run *very* fast," said Monty.

"I know," said Dilly, worried. She stared hard at the rushing water, foaming and bubbling over the mossy boulders beneath the bridge. "I wouldn't want to swim in that!"

Dilly was very nervous of the river even when the water was still and calm.

"It scares me." Dilly shivered. "But it doesn't scare Racer!"

"I'm going to wait at the finish line," said Socks, running towards the Old Tree Stump. "That's the most exciting bit."

Suddenly, Dilly saw a little black duckling shoot out from under the bridge's arch. It was Racer!

Dilly took off, waddling quickly along the river bank as Racer practised his tricky twists and turns.

"Go Racer, go!" Dilly quacked encouragement from the sidelines. Racer glanced up from the river and waved a wing.

From the safety of the shore, Dilly kept up with the practice as Racer zipped around the first obstacle: Tulip Bend. Then she held her breath, her heart fluttering in her chest, as he swam through the second: Bulrush Pass.

Dilly's feathers stood on end as she imagined how it might feel, swimming through such a dark, black tunnel. Racer would struggle to see where he was going and he might feel lonely in there all on his own.

"Hoorah!" cheered Dilly as Racer sailed safely out of the rushes. Then it was the third and final obstacle: Rock Falls, the trickiest part of the course.

The river twisted and turned and dipped down a slope. The water churned angrily over the rocks and Dilly felt dizzy just thinking about swimming through all the bends, turning this way and that.

She reached the Old Tree Stump ahead of Racer and joined Socks at the finish line. Rock Falls rushed and foamed fiercely.

"The river looks like it's boiling," said Socks. He peered into the water and shook his head. "Better Racer than me," commented the little piglet.

Dilly glanced back towards the Gushing Gap – a shorter route over the Falls between two giant stones. She shivered. The water churned angrily. No one had ever swum through the Gap. No one, except Dilly's granddad.

"Look, here comes Racer!" Dilly gasped as her brother bobbed and weaved his way through the falls.

"Watch out!" cried Dilly. Racer had made a wrong turn and almost crashed into a rock. Luckily, he veered left at the last moment, and burst through the foam.

Dilly let out a little cheer as Racer crossed the finish line.

"Do you think YOU might ever enter the Feather Race?" asked Socks, looking Dilly up and down. "Racer can't be the only good swimmer in the family."

"Oh, noooo!" quacked Dilly. "I couldn't. It's all far too scary for me. I can't race like Racer. Not one bit!" Dilly didn't like to draw attention to herself. It had always been the same. With so many brothers and sisters, Dilly had found it difficult to make her voice heard. And then that scary fox had bitten off part of her tail, which had made her ever so nervous. No, it was much better to stay in the background.

Dilly's family waddled over from the barn, laughing and calling out. Dilly's brothers and sisters swarmed round her, ruffling her feathers and jostling her cheerfully.

Racer jumped out of the river and shook his feathers, showering Dilly with cold water droplets.

"Did you see me take that last bend?" he asked, gasping for breath.

"You were brilliant," said Dilly. "You were really fantastic, Racer. I bet you'll beat Silver's grandson, Swift, and Goldie's granddaughter, Glory, by miles. Racer will win back the Golden Feather trophy for the ducks." Dilly took a deep gulp of air. She couldn't remember the last time she'd said so much all at once!

Dilly's brothers and sisters cheered, flapping their wings as they jumped up and down.

"I can't wait for the big day," quacked Racer. "But I don't know if I'm really fast enough to win the race. Swift the cygnet is very powerful. And Goldie has enormous paddles for feet!"

"It's the taking part that counts," Mum said. "Not the winning." She lay a wing across Racer's gleaming feathers. "Just swim like a Darefeather," she said. "And that will be good enough." Dilly watched as her mum and her granddad, Drake, shared a glance. They looked very proud. All the other ducklings cheered, stamping their feet and flapping their wings as they jumped up and down.

Mum smiled, then nudged Dilly and the others gently with her bill. They walked back home along the path to Pebble Pond. Dilly walked next to her granddad, Drake.

"I wish I could be a proper Darefeather, like Racer," Dilly said. Her granddad stroked the soft feathers on the top of Dilly's head.

"You already are a proper Darefeather," Drake said, as he hobbled along. His old legs weren't as strong as they used to be.

"Do you think so?" asked Dilly. She couldn't imagine a time when she might feel brave.

"Of course I do," said Drake, as the two of them walked towards the Big Red Barn. "You just need to believe in yourself. Everyone else does." Dilly looked up at her granddad. He sounded as if he meant it. Drake Darefeather really thought Dilly could be brave.

Chapter Three

Early morning the following day was bright and sunny. Dilly was about to go and watch Racer, Swift and Glory practising again on the river, when her friends, Parsley and Smudge, came bounding up to her in the farmyard.

"You've just got to come up to Great Oak Hill," woofed Smudge.

"Farmer Rob left a hose running when he was filling Oscar's trough," explained Parsley. "And now there's a long, wet, grassy strip on the hill and everyone's sliding down it."

"Show me the way!" Dilly quacked. Watching her friends slide down the hill sounded like fun! Her webbed feet made loud smacking noises on the cobbles as she ran behind her friends, out of the farmyard and up the hill. They came to a stop at the top of the green hill. A path of wet grass and water streaked down the hill, glinting in the sunlight. It looked *very* slippery.

Dilly watched as Smudge took a long run at the wet grass. Then he flipped himself on to his rear end, and skidded along the water slide right to the bottom of the hill. Smudge yapped all the way down.

"That looks fantastic!" cried Dilly.

Now it was Parsley's turn. The little Jack Russell took a flying leap on to her round tummy. She spread her legs out to the sides. Dilly laughed as Parsley surfed all the way to the bottom.

Her friends were having a great time.

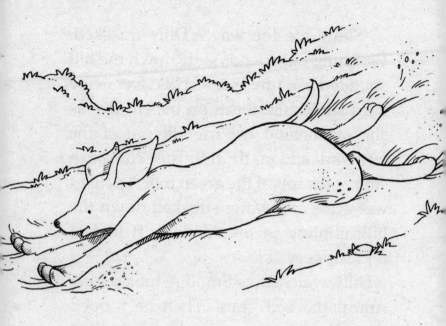

And the wet slide looked so cool in the morning heat. Could she? Dilly reached out a foot, about to take a step closer to the water slide. Then she hesitated. What if she hurt herself? And her friends would be watching. Dilly wasn't sure she could cope with all those eyes on her. Dilly quickly pulled her foot back in, but it was too late. Smudge had spotted what she'd been doing.

"Come and have a go," suggested Smudge.

Dilly shook her head. "It's far too fast for me. What if I tumble over?" Part of Dilly wanted to join in, but she didn't feel she could let herself go. Her heart hammered in her chest just thinking about whizzing down the hill.

It looks brilliant, she thought. *But…*

Granddad Drake waddled over. "Why don't you take a turn?" he asked, gently nudging her towards the slide.

"*Quack!*" Dilly jumped back in alarm. "I can't. I can't possibly," she insisted.

"But this isn't scary!" Her granddad smiled. "It looks like fun. If I was a bit younger, I'd be straight down there. Why not try?"

Dilly glanced around as Monty and Ernest threw themselves down the water slide together, rushing past with giggles and squawks of delight. A question nibbled at the back of Dilly's mind.

Could her granddad be right? Could she at least try the water slide? Smudge and Parsley were having such fun.

"Come on, Dilly," panted Parsley, as she ran back up the hill. "Why don't you take it slowly and try a little skid?"

"And don't worry," said Drake. "You don't have to go fast. Just start halfway. Nice and slow. I promise to stay close by and nudge you along if you need it."

Dilly thought about it. Then she thought about it some more. Then she got to her feet. This was possibly the bravest thing Dilly had ever done in her life.

"OK," said Dilly. "I'll have a go."

She ruffled her feathers and waddled halfway up the edge of the water slide.

"Go, Dilly!" cried Smudge.

Dilly stepped on to the wet patch of grass. First one webbed foot. Then the other. The grass felt very wet and squidgy underfoot. And VERY slippery.

"I don't think I like this!" said Dilly. She could hear that her voice had gone very high and tight.

"Don't be scared," said Drake soothingly. "You're quite safe." He leant over to give her a gentle push with his beak and – wheeeeeeeee! Dilly began to slide.

She felt the grass sliding beneath her feet. She kept her wings close to her body as she tried not to fall over. But everything was happening so quickly that she didn't have time to get *really* scared.

"Go, Dilly, go!" cried Parsley.

Before she knew it, she had slid all the way to the bottom. Dilly stepped off the water slide and cocked her head on one side as she tried to work out how she felt. She didn't feel like bursting into tears. And she couldn't feel her legs trembling. She was fine.

In fact, she was better than fine. She'd enjoyed going fast. She looked back up the hill at her friends waving at her. She knew what she had to do next. She had to have another go!

"That was fun!" cried Dilly, waddling back up the hill.

As she caught up with her friends, she preened her chest feathers with her bill. "This time," she announced, "I want to do it all on my own."

She waddled to the top of the hill. The very top.

24

"She's going to do it!" whispered Monty.

The water slide shimmered in the bright sunlight. Dilly looked down the hill. She had never seen the grass look so green. From this distance, Dilly could see Willow River. She was very high up. Dilly's legs began to wobble.

But then she spotted Racer down below, practising his fast turns on the river bend. Her courage returned.

"Right. Here goes," quacked Dilly. She took a deep breath then ran at the slide as fast as she could. Dilly spread her wings for balance as she leapt on to the wet patch and surfed all the way down from top to bottom. The wind rushed through her feathers. The trees whizzed past her wings. And the slippery, green grass tickled her feet.

"Wheeeeee! That was amazing." Dilly jumped up and down, squelching her feet in the wet grass. She felt really pleased with herself. "Going fast isn't really scary after all," said Dilly. "It's brilliant!" She looked around, beaming as her friends cheered. Dilly didn't at all mind being the centre of attention.

"Well done, Dilly Darefeather," cried Drake. "You could do it all along!"

Chapter Four

The next day after lunch, Dilly, Socks and Parsley decided to go for a walk.

"Don't go further than the Old Tree Stump," said Dilly's mum, giving Dilly a kiss on the top of her head. "And keep out of mischief."

The friends chased each other out of the barn doors. They passed by the edge of Albert Wood. Tall trees grew close together, forming a shady canopy of leafy branches. Dilly could see pretty dappled sunlight filtering down on to the woodland floor.

"Look!" Socks had spotted a wild blueberry bush full of plump, ripe blueberries, nestling between the nearest trees. The berries glistened, fat and tempting, in the dappled shade.

"I think we've just found an afternoon snack!" said the piglet. The three friends ran over. Dilly reached out her beak and plucked a fat berry off the bush. It burst in her mouth and she swallowed the tasty juice. These were the best berries Dilly had eaten all summer. Her bill was soon dripping with purple juice as she pecked another berry and another berry straight off the bush.

"*Mmm!* These are deeelicious," mumbled Socks through a mouthful of berries.

Soon, all the blueberries hanging from the lower branches of the bush were gone. Dilly, Socks and Parsley had gobbled the lot.

"There are plenty more up there," said Dilly, pointing at the topmost branches with her wing. "But how can we reach them?"

She tried jumping, but couldn't reach very high. Parsley tried, but the bush was a bit prickly and scratched her nose.

Then Socks had an idea. "Maybe Parsley can jump up on to my back and bring all the berries down!"

Dilly thought it sounded like a great plan.

Parsley took a deep breath – and then jumped! But instead of making it up on to Socks's back, Parsley knocked him over, sending them both sprawling.

"Sorry about that, Socks," Parsley said.

"That didn't work, did it?" Socks said, shaking himself off.

"How about plan B?" said Parsley.

"What's that?" asked Dilly and Socks together.

Parsley explained. "Socks stands up and YOU, Dilly, flap up on to his head. From there you can easily hop on and off the top branches and pass the berries down."

"Whaaaaaaaat?" quacked Dilly. "Up there?" She shook her head. "No way. I can't. I can't possibly. It's far too high. What if I fall off the branch and tumble into the prickly bush? It's too scary. I could get hurt!"

"That's true!" Socks said, winking at Parsley.

"And we don't want you to do anything that scares you," teased Parsley. Dilly didn't mind being teased by her friends. But she'd love to show them they were wrong. She looked up at the juicy berries again.

It would be nice to eat a few more, she thought. Dilly remembered what Granddad Drake had said to her. She just had to believe in herself...

I'll do it! thought Dilly.

"Come on, you two," announced Dilly. "Let's give it a try!"

Socks stood up on his hind legs. His corkscrew tail twirled and twitched as he concentrated on not falling over. Dilly gulped and flapped awkwardly up on to his head.

"Whoahh!" Dilly held out her wings for balance and tried to steady herself. Socks was swaying from one leg to the other, trying to help. But that only seemed to make things worse. Dilly was wobbling up there on the top of his head like a jelly.

"Oh, no. I don't like this," she quacked. She was a long way off the ground and if Socks fell over, Dilly could see that she would land with a real thump.

Then she found that if she concentrated really hard and lowered her wings a little, she

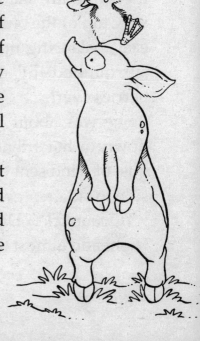

felt quite steady. She had found her balance!

"Well done, Dilly," cried Parsley. "You're terrific!"

Dilly jumped on to the nearest branch. The branch bent slightly under her weight.

Oh, no! Are the branches strong enough to hold me? For a second, Dilly was worried. But … yes! The branches were bendy, but strong. Dilly relaxed and hopped up on to another branch. Then another – even higher, until she was perched on the very top of the blueberry bush. It wasn't easy, balancing up there, but Dilly was surrounded by the biggest, juiciest berries ever!

She was about to start passing them down to her friends, when suddenly a gust of wind sent the bush swaying from side to side.

"Quaarrrck!" Dilly gave a squawk of fright and almost toppled off the branch.

"Keep calm, Dilly. You can do it!" called Parsley.

Dilly shifted her weight from left to right as the branch swayed.

Left… Right. Left… Right. Balance with your wings.

"There you go, Dilly," oinked Socks. "You're doing it!"

"I am. I am!" quacked Dilly with delight. "I'm balancing. Look at me. I'm balancing!"

"We knew you could do it all along," yapped Parsley.

Dilly puffed out her chest. She felt so pleased with herself, balancing high in the blueberry bush. She dropped berry after berry down to her friends on the ground below.

"The only thing that could top how happy I feel right now," said Dilly. "Would be if the ducks win the Golden Feather Trophy tomorrow morning!"

Chapter Five

Trumpet the Old English sheepdog came bounding past. He stopped and gazed up at Dilly in amazement. Dilly looked down, spread her wings and balanced expertly on the topmost branches of the bush.

"Look at you, Dilly! Quite the daredevil," Trumpet said.

"Quite the Darefeather, you mean!" said Dilly happily.

"There's been a call for a last minute practice run down at the river," announced Trumpet. "Everyone's going down there to watch." He dashed off towards the river.

"Come on," Socks called up to Dilly. "Let's go!"

Dilly flapped her way down to the ground and raced with her two friends along to Willow River.

Dilly's granddad was on the river bank. He was surrounded by a crowd of fluffy ducklings. They had all come to shout encouragement to Racer as he sped through the last practice run before the big race.

"Hello there, Dilly," said Drake, as she went to sit down next to him. The ducklings moved to one side to make room for her.

Dilly could see Racer swimming down the river towards them. She was so proud of her brother – he really knew what he was doing. Even Drake gasped as Racer zipped round Tulip Bend, taking the faster, inside edge, against the rushing current. Racer was flying along. He kept low in the water and turned at the last possible moment.

"Well done, Racer," called Drake. "That's my boy!"

"Racer! Racer! Racer!" Dilly and the other ducklings cheered.

Dilly held her breath as her brother swam into Bulrush Pass and disappeared from view. Dilly didn't like that part of the course. Bulrush Pass was a long tunnel of reeds and overhanging trees. It was very dark in there, thick with weeds and hidden tree roots. Dilly imagined the rushing current pushing Racer faster and faster as he dodged through the dark, scary tunnel.

Dilly held her breath as she waited for Racer to emerge from the bulrushes. Where was he? He seemed to be taking a long time – too long. Dilly looked up nervously at Drake. He was shaking his head slowly.

"Don't worry," Drake murmured. "He'll be fine." But Drake's eyes were fixed on the bulrushes.

"Racer should have swum clear by now!" Dilly blurted out. She got to her feet and ran down to the bank of the river. She craned her neck out and tried to peer among the thick stalks. Nothing. She couldn't see a thing.

Suddenly Dilly heard her brother cry out in pain. Then he emerged, swimming awkwardly with his leg trailing behind him near the surface of the water. He struggled to swim to the shore.

Racer was injured! And as the strong current of the river rushed past him, Dilly could see that he was struggling to get to the bank. Racer was going to be swept away – unless someone did something. Racer looked up at her and as their eyes locked, Dilly knew exactly what she had to do.

"Don't worry!" she called out to her brother.

Dilly didn't waste a second. She jumped straight into the river to help her brother.

As she hit the water, Dilly gasped. It was cold! She could feel the strong pull of the current under the surface, trying to drag her away. Dilly felt a stab of fear.

But then she saw Racer, up ahead, fighting against the current. No way was she going to leave her brother out there in the river on his own.

All the other ducklings stared – open billed – as Dilly swam over to Racer. She pushed against the water with her webbed feet using long, strong strokes. It was hard work, but Racer looked so lost and helpless. She had to get to him. With a final surge of energy she caught up with him.

"My leg!" Racer panted. Dilly didn't have time to reply. She swam behind him and started to push him back towards the bank.

"Are you OK?" called Trumpet, jumping into the shallows to help.

"I got trapped by a tree root in the pass," groaned Racer. "The water was rushing so fast I didn't see it lurking below the surface."

Trumpet used his nose to help Dilly

nudge Racer safely back up on to the dry bank. Racer's leg hung limply behind him. "It hurts," he quacked softly.

Dilly hopped out of the river and shook droplets of water from her wings. Then, Dilly realized what she'd done. She had just plunged feet first into the river past White Stone Bridge! Dilly had rescued her brother and swum in one of the most difficult parts of the river.

Racer hobbled painfully up the bank. "Thanks, sis," he said, giving Dilly a peck on the cheek.

Old Spotty stood in the dappled shade of a tree shaking her head slowly from side to side. Dilly realized she must have been watching everything.

"Oh dear, what an awful shame," she said. "And Racer was showing so much promise for the ducks as well!"

Dilly tilted her head to one side, puzzled.

"There's no way that Racer can swim

in the Feather Race with his leg hurt like that," Old Spotty said.

"What?" Dilly couldn't believe it.

"I'm OK, really," insisted Racer. "It's nothing. Only a little sprain." He tried bravely to stand on his own, but his leg gave way beneath him.

"Owwww!" He stuck out a wing, trying to regain his balance.

"You see," said Old Spotty. "There is NO WAY you will be fit enough to race tomorrow, Racer."

Drake gently took Racer aside.

"I'm afraid Old Spotty is right," said Drake. "It would be very foolish to even think of racing with an injured leg."

Dilly wondered if Racer was going to cry. But he didn't. Everyone fell silent as he lifted his head and struggled to keep his eyes dry.

"OK," he said, puffing out his little downy chest. "I understand. And I officially withdraw from the race."

Dilly felt a big lump in her throat as she followed the animals back into the Big Red Barn.

Old Spotty quickly gathered everyone together for an emergency race meeting. She stood on top of a big wooden box. "Due to an untimely injury, Racer the duckling is unable to compete in tomorrow's race," she announced.

Dilly heard all the animals around her gasp in shock. She couldn't look round at them – she didn't want to see their faces.

"It would be unfair to continue the race without an entry from the ducks," continued Old Spotty. "So, I am afraid that this year's Willow River Feather Race, is hereby ... CANCELLED."

Chapter Six

No one could believe it. Dilly stood with Socks and Parsley by the stalls, at the back of the barn. She couldn't imagine how Racer must be feeling. This would be the first year that Little Bridge Farm had been without the Feather Race. It was so disappointing.

Dilly watched Oscar walk slowly over. He lowered his head to the ground and whispered quietly in her ear.

"The Feather Race could still go ahead if YOU took your brother's place," he said.

45

"Who, me?" Dilly was shocked. "No. No, I couldn't possibly." She glanced across at Racer, sitting on a bed of straw.

"I – I couldn't hurt his feelings," said Dilly. "Besides," she quacked, "I've never swum the course before. And all those animals watching – I couldn't!" Dilly's skin went prickly just thinking about it.

"But you know every bit of Willow River," said Oscar. "And you know the course like the back of your wing.

All you've got to do is believe in yourself, and you can do it!"

"No, no, it's impossible," said Dilly. "I'm not half the swimmer that Racer is." She waddled quickly away into Filbert's empty stall.

Suddenly, Dilly felt something tickle her ear. A white feather! She spun around and there was her friend, Ernest the goose. He'd followed her into the pen.

"Go on, Dilly," he urged. "You're a much better swimmer than you think you are, and you'll enjoy everyone watching and cheering you on."

Monty the moorhen ducked through a gap from the neighbouring stall.

"Look how you dived in and helped Racer swim back to the bank," said Monty. "It takes a strong swimmer to do that."

Smudge poked his head round the stall-gate. "I'm sure Racer could talk you through the course."

"He knows all the tricky twists and turns," said Socks. All Dilly's friends had followed her into the pen.

"And you've got m-m-much bigger feet than R-R-Racer," pointed out Filbert.

Dilly swallowed hard. She'd been really brave in the past few days. She wondered ... just maybe she could swim in the race she loved so much.

"And just think how excited everyone will be," yapped Parsley, "if the race were to be back on."

Dilly took an enormous breath. She decided right then that she was going to do it. Now it was time to ask Racer and her mum if it was all right for her to swim in Racer's place.

Dilly waddled out of the stall with all her friends following behind. Mum was sitting near Racer on his bed of straw. They both looked up, surprised, as Dilly and her group of friends walked over to them. Dilly took a big breath. It was now or never.

"Would it be OK if I took Racer's place and swam for the ducks in the Feather Race?" she asked.

Dilly's mum looked surprised. "But you've always been so nervous of the river," she said. "And so shy!"

"But I don't want to be afraid any more," quacked Dilly. "I've done other things that I've always been scared of doing. And now, I want to swim for the ducks in the Willow River Feather Race! Even if it does mean people watching me." She looked at her brother. Racer looked at Dilly. Then he turned his head and hobbled away on his injured leg.

"Oh, dear," said Dilly, worried. She turned back to look at her mum. But then she heard Racer quack loudly for everyone to listen. Racer was standing on the big box next to Old Spotty.

"I am delighted to announce," he

exclaimed, "that my brilliant sister, Dilly, is taking my place, and will be swimming tomorrow for the ducks." He caught Dilly's eye and gave her a wink.

All the animals went wild – whooping and cheering with excitement.

"Good old Dilly!"

"Go, ducks, go!"

"I suppose this means that the race is back on," grunted Old Spotty with a half smile. "I *do* wish people would make up their minds!"

That evening, when Dilly was tucked up in her nest, she worried whether she was really up to being in the race after all.

"Maybe I just got carried away by everyone's enthusiasm," she said to herself. *What if I get injured like Racer?* she thought. *I was quite brave today. But out there? On the river?*

Dilly began to have second thoughts.

But then she remembered how good it felt once she had conquered her fear of the water slide. And all that fun with the blueberry bush!

"That was brilliant!" quacked Dilly out loud. She looked around, hoping she hadn't woken the others. Everyone was still sleeping. But her grandfather, Drake Darefeather, stirred. He peered into the nest.

"I just want to wish you good luck for tomorrow," he whispered. "And to tell you how proud we all are of you."

Dilly felt a warm glow fill her up inside.

"If swimming in the race can make me feel THIS good," said Dilly. "It has to be worth it. Tomorrow, I'm going to give it everything I've got!"

"And just remember," whispered Drake. "Trust yourself, Dilly." He kissed Dilly goodnight. "I'll be with you all the way."

Chapter Seven

It rained again during the night. But the next morning the grey clouds parted and the sky was bright blue. The river had never looked so fast as it rushed and bubbled beneath the stone arch of the bridge.

Dilly gulped as she stood under the bridge and peered at the raging water below. Swift the cygnet didn't seem bothered. He just stood there preening his feathers. And Glory the gosling didn't bat an eyelid. She was casually flexing her enormous paddles and doing her warm-up exercises.

Dilly tried not to worry.

All the animals from Little Bridge Farm were crowded along the river bank, lining the course of the race. Dilly tried not to think about how many animals would be watching her today.

"Contestants," called Old Spotty in her best official voice. "Line up, on your blocks!"

The three contestants for the annual Willow River Feather Race took up their positions beneath the bridge. Each bird stood on a mossy boulder. Dilly looked ahead. The river foamed over her webbed feet. And she felt afraid. She looked around and spotted Racer and the rest of her family. They were cheering her name.

"Dilly! Dilly! Dilly!"

I'm going to do this for all my family and friends! she thought.

Trumpet gave the starting bark – "Woof, woof!" – and the race was on.

Dilly leaped off the starting stone. She could hear the animals calling out as she paddled furiously along the first leg of the race. Dilly was swimming as fast as she could, but Swift and Glory were already ahead.

Tulip Bend seemed to come out of nowhere. Dilly saw Swift cut across Glory at the turn and Glory quickly swerved aside to avoid a collision.

This meant Dilly was going to have to take the sharper, faster bend. She hadn't been expecting that at all.

"Whoa!" Dilly had never taken a corner so fast before – but she loved it! Feet paddling, she leaned into the bank as the current pulled her round.

"Dilly! Dilly! Dilly!" the crowd chanted as she stormed along the next part of the course, zipping and darting between rocks and ducking under low branches. Swift and Glory were still ahead, but Dilly was catching up.

Bulrush Pass loomed ahead. This was where Racer had his accident! Dilly didn't have time to worry about how dark and dangerous the tunnel might be. She plunged head first into the dense pass.

The tunnel of reeds surrounded her. Their stems scratched against her sides as she paddled through. She could feel thick weeds below the water. It was dark, but Dilly could see a light ahead.

"Watch out for roots," she heard Racer yell.

Dilly pushed her feet as far out behind her as possible, and lay as low as she could on the water. She kicked her paddles slowly and calmly with a smooth, powerful action.

Keep calm, Dilly. Keep calm.

Dilly was moving really fast. She burst out of the tunnel into the sunshine – the first swimmer through the pass!

A flash of white feathers caught Dilly's eye. She glanced sideways as Swift pulled alongside.

Wow, he's fast! she thought. Only a few of the animals lined the river this far down the course, but they still called out encouragement. "Go, Dilly! Go, Swift!"

Who would be the winner?

The young swan lowered his long, graceful neck and surged forwards. As he swept past Dilly he turned and gave her a wink – as if he was sure he was going to win the race. "See you at the finish line!" Swift panted, before pushing on ahead.

Dilly paddled even faster. He wasn't going to get away with that! But Dilly was tiring now and Glory was passing her. Rock Falls lay ahead.

Dilly glanced at the bank. Drake was there, running along the side to keep up with her. Seeing Drake gave Dilly an extra spurt. She zipped forwards and began to slalom between the rocks. It was neck-and-neck, beak-to-bill, as the three birds swam as fast as they possibly could. Dilly's leg muscles were aching but she was determined to try her hardest and finish the race, even if she couldn't win it.

"Go, Dilly! Go!" The crowd was whooping Dilly's name. It was fantastic. Their voices urged her on.

Dilly surged forwards, swerving and weaving her way through the treacherous course. All the rain had made this the fastest race EVER!

The end of Rock Falls and the finish line lay directly ahead. Dilly was tired. Swift the cygnet was a much bigger bird. Slowly, he pulled ahead again.

How could Dilly win the race now?

They were almost at the end of the course. Swift was in the lead, passing Gushing Gap and about to take the final bend to the finish line. Dilly could see that the river rushed much faster between the Gap's two giant stones. It looked really scary. But it was a quicker route. Only one bird had ever swum through the Gap.

Only one bird, ever!

What should Dilly do?

She glanced up quickly to the bank. Drake Darefeather stood by the giant stones. One quick nod of his head was enough.

"Here goes!" Dilly called out.

Dilly shut her eyes tight and hurled herself between the two giant stones, through the Gushing Gap. The water foamed over her head as she went under. Dilly felt herself rolling over in the water.

Dilly struggled to straighten up, and paddled as hard as she could. Then, there was a massive cheer as Dilly shot out of the other side, ahead of Swift, and zipped past the finish line at the Old Tree Stump to take first place.

"YIPPEEEEEEEE!"

Dilly Darefeather had won the Feather Race for the ducks!

Dilly hopped out of the water and up on to the bank. She couldn't believe it. Everyone rushed down to the river bank to congratulate her. But Dilly only had one thing on her mind. She pushed through the crowd of well-wishers to reach her brother. Racer hobbled forwards and threw his little wings around her neck.

"Three cheers for our champion, Dilly," he cried.

"Who isn't afraid of anything!" added Drake.

"Dilly! Dilly! Dilly!" Smudge and Parsley began to chant, as all her friends and family cheered. Dilly's chest puffed out. This was even better than the water slide! Dilly never dreamed she'd be able to join in the Feather Race, let alone win it – but look what she could do when she tried!

"Well done, Dilly Darefeather," said Drake.

"I'm so proud of you," added Dilly's mum, as she waddled over.

Dilly had never felt happier in her life as she made her way up to the presentation platform – a big, flat rock, raised high above the river bank.

All the other ducklings rushed forwards, cheering as she passed.

"Go, Dilly! Go!" shouted Ernest. Even

Swift and Glory were pleased for Dilly.

"You were fast," said Glory.

"VERY fast," added Swift. "And to brave the Gushing Gap like that ... well ... absolutely AMAZING!"

Old Spotty the pig bellowed for silence as Dilly climbed up on to the winner's podium. Then more cheers rang out as Old Spotty produced the winner's trophy – a beautiful, golden feather.

"It gives me great pleasure," announced Old Spotty, "to present this year's award to the ducks, and their brilliant swimmer – winner of the Willow River Feather Race – Dilly Darefeather!"

Dilly felt so proud of herself as she looked at all the happy faces around her. *I could learn to like this attention*, she thought to herself. She had proved that she was as good as anyone else. All she had to do was believe in herself!

Dilly climbed down off the podium to lead all the animals in a procession, back to Big Red Barn. It had been an amazing race!

"What's your next challenge going to be?" asked Oscar as he clip-clopped over the cobblestones next to Dilly. Dilly laughed.

"I don't know," she said. "But whatever it is, I'll be ready for it."

Look out for the rest of the series!

Oscar's New Friends

Little Bridge Farm was bathed in golden light as the setting sun disappeared slowly behind Great Oak Hill.

Oscar – a young chestnut pony – glanced nervously at the Big Red Barn. Then he looked around at the empty meadows. Beyond the farmhouse, he could see a dark forest and green rolling hills. It was all new to him. He looked back at Suzy, his very best friend, and blew a desperate whinny.

Suzy threw her arms around Oscar's neck and gave him one last goodbye hug. Oscar knew that Suzy was trying to be brave for his sake, but he could still hear her snuffles as she struggled not to cry. Suzy and Oscar had always been best friends and now he was saying goodbye to her – for ever.

Oscar nudged his velvet muzzle against Suzy's cheek and whickered softly. Then he looked up and saw the tears rolling down her face.

Oscar whinnied sadly.

Suzy rubbed her eyes and sobbed. "I hope you'll be happy here, Oscar. Farmer Rob is a very nice man. And I know he'll look after you really well."

Oscar gazed down at the ground. Suzy wouldn't be able to visit him any more. She used to visit him three days a week at the Big City Stables. Suzy had explained to Oscar that her family was moving away. Her dad had been given an important job abroad, and they couldn't take a pony with them. Oscar knew Suzy would find him a good new home, but his heart still ached at the thought of saying goodbye.

Farmer Rob Newberry gently took hold of Oscar's halter as Suzy's mum led her away to the waiting car.

Oscar neighed sadly. His ears lay flat against his head as he pawed the soft earth with his hooves.

"I'll always love you," called Suzy.

And I'll never forget you, Oscar thought, as he whickered a last goodbye. Giant tears rolled from the pony's eyes. Even though Oscar wasn't a baby any more, he was still very young, and he had never felt so frightened or lonely in his entire life. He watched the family car drive slowly away, over the little stone bridge, back to the Big City. And his heart broke.

"Goodbye, Suzy," he said, as the car turned a corner and disappeared for ever.

Oscar looked up at the sky. The moon was coming out from behind some clouds, but it was very dark here in the countryside.

Where are all the bright lights? he thought.

It was very quiet as well. Not like the Big City. He was used to hearing cars whizzing along all night. But then there was something – a strange hooting sound Oscar had never heard before. The little pony pricked up his ears.

"What was that?" Oscar snorted. He felt a bit scared.

"Steady, young fella," said Farmer Rob soothingly. He rubbed Oscar's neck.

Oscar looked around nervously as Farmer Rob led him by his halter rope.

Farmer Rob stopped at the Big Red Barn and swung open the huge wooden doors. Oscar gave a little swallow and looked inside. This barn was enormous. And it was very dark and spooky!

The farmer flicked on the light switch and filled the barn with a soft, amber glow. Wooden beams and criss-crossed rafters held up the vast roof which towered above Oscar's head. He looked up, feeling dizzy. Oscar had never been inside such a huge, roomy place before. His stable in the Big City had been quite small. And a little cramped. Oscar used to share his stall with haughty Harriet, a thoroughbred hunter.

At the end of the big barn was a row of four wooden stalls. Oscar could see that there were other animals inside three of them: two great big ones, and a scrawny, scrappy one.

Oscar hesitated. He placed one foot gingerly on the sawdust which covered the floor. But then Farmer Rob clapped him lightly on the rump, and Oscar trotted inside his new, empty stall.

"There you are, Oscar," said the farmer. "That wasn't too bad, was it?"

Oscar hadn't decided yet. He shook out his mane and tried to look at the animals in the other stalls. Although he couldn't see them clearly, he was almost certain that they were squinting back at him. Oscar hoped they would

be friendlier than the snooty Big City ponies – especially haughty Harriet.

Oscar felt the warmth of the barn through his thick, chestnut coat. Then he spotted something in the corner. It was a mother dog with her tiny, newborn puppies snuggling up against her pink belly. They all looked so happy together and Oscar felt himself slowly relax.

Perhaps I could be happy here, too, he thought.